TIMOLEON

by
Herman Melville

LITERATURE HOUSE / GREGG PRESS
Upper Saddle River, N. J.

Republished in 1970 by
LITERATURE HOUSE
an imprint of The Gregg Press
121 Pleasant Avenue
Upper Saddle River, N. J. 07458

Standard Book Number—8398-1255-8
Library of Congress Card—74-104526

Printed in United States of America

TIMOLEON

ETC.

NEW YORK
THE CAXTON PRESS
1891

TO

MY COUNTRYMAN

ELIHU VEDDER

TABLE OF CONTENTS.

TIMOLEON.

(394 B. C.)

I.

IF more than once, as annals tell,
   Through blood without compunction spilt,
An egotist arch rule has snatched
And stamped the seizure with his sabre's hilt,
   And, legalized by lawyers, stood ;
Shall the good heart whose patriot fire
Leaps to a deed of startling note,
Do it, then flinch ? Shall good in weak expire ?
   Needs goodness lack the evil grit
That stares down censorship and ban,
And dumfounds saintlier ones with this—
God's will avouched in each successful man ?
   Or, put it, where dread stress inspires
A virtue beyond man's standard rate,
Seems virtue there a strain forbid—

Transcendence such as shares transgression's fate?
  If so, and wan eclipse ensue,
Yet glory await emergence won,
Is that high Providence, or Chance?
And proved it which with thee, Timoleon?
  O, crowned with laurel twined with thorn,
Not rash thy life's cross-tide I stem,
But reck the problem rolled in pang
And reach and dare to touch thy garment's hem.

II.

  When Argos and Cleone strove
Against free Corinth's claim or right,
Two brothers battled for her well:
A footman one, and one a mounted knight.
  Apart in place, each braved the brunt
Till the rash cavalryman, alone,
Was wrecked against the enemy's files,
His bayard crippled and he maimed and thrown.
  Timoleon, at Timophanes' need,
Makes for the rescue through the fray,
Covers him with his shield, and takes
The darts and furious odds and fights at bay;
  Till, wrought to palor of passion dumb,
Stark terrors of death around he throws,

Warding his brother from the field
Spite failing friends dispersed and rallying foes.
   Here might he rest, in claim rest here,
Rest, and a Phidian form remain;
But life halts never, life must on,
And take with term prolonged some scar or stain.
   Yes, life must on. And latent germs
Time's seasons wake in mead and man;
And brothers, playfellows in youth,
Develop into variance wide in span.

III.

   Timophanes was his mother's pride—
Her pride, her pet, even all to her
Who slackly on Timoleon looked:
Scarce he (she mused) may proud affection stir.
   He saved my darling, gossips tell:
If so, 'twas service, yea, and fair;
But instinct ruled and duty bade,
In service such, a henchman e'en might share.
   When boys they were I helped the bent;
I made the junior feel his place,
Subserve the senior, love him, too;
And sooth he does, and that's his saving grace.
   But me the meek one never can serve,

Not he, he lacks the quality keen
To make the mother through the son
An envied dame of power, a social queen.
    But thou, my first-born, thou art I
In sex translated; joyed, I scan
My features, mine, expressed in thee;
Thou art what I would be were I a man.
    My brave Timophanes, 'tis thou
Who yet the world's fore-front shalt win,
For thine the urgent resolute way,
Self pushing panoplied self through thick and
    thin.
    Nor here maternal insight erred:
Foresworn, with heart that did not wince
At slaying men who kept their vows,
Her darling strides to power, and reigns—a
    Prince.

IV.

    Because of just heart and humane,
Profound the hate Timoleon knew
For crimes of pride and men-of-prey
And impious deeds that perjurous upstarts do;
    And Corinth loved he, and in way
Old Scotia's clansman loved his clan,

Devotion one with ties how dear
And passion that late to make the rescue ran.
 But crime and kin—the terrorized town,
The silent, acquiescent mother—
Revulsion racks the filial heart,
The loyal son, the patriot true, the brother.
 In evil visions of the night
He sees the lictors of the gods,
Giant ministers of righteousness,
Their *fasces* threatened by the Furies' rods.
 But undeterred he wills to act,
Resolved thereon though Ate rise;
He heeds the voice whose mandate calls,
Or seems to call, peremptory from the skies.

V.

 Nor less but by approaches mild,
And trying each prudential art,
The just one first advances him
In parley with a flushed intemperate heart.
 The brother first he seeks—alone,
And pleads; but is with laughter met;
Then comes he, in accord with two,
And these adjure the tyrant and beset;
 Whose merriment gives place to rage:

"Go," stamping, "what to me is Right?
I am the Wrong, and lo, I reign,
And testily intolerant too in might:"
   And glooms on his mute brother pale,
Who goes aside; with muffled face
He sobs the predetermined word,
And Right in Corinth reassumes its place.

VI.

   But on his robe, ah, whose the blood?
And craven ones their eyes avert,
And heavy is a mother's ban,
And dismal faces of the fools can hurt.
   The whispering-gallery of the world,
Where each breathed slur runs wheeling wide
Eddies a false perverted truth,
Inveterate turning still on fratricide.
   The time was Plato's. Wandering lights
Confirmed the atheist's standing star;
As now, no sanction Virtue knew
For deeds that on prescriptive morals jar.
   Reaction took misgiving's tone,
Infecting conscience, till betrayed
To doubt the irrevocable doom
Herself had authorized when undismayed.

Within perturbed Timoleon here
Such deeps were bared as when the sea
Convulsed, vacates its shoreward bed,
And Nature's last reserves show nakedly.
  He falters, and from Hades' glens
By night insidious tones implore—
Why suffer? hither come and be
What Phocion is who feeleth man no more.
  But, won from that, his mood elects
To live—to live in wilding place;
For years self-outcast, he but meets
In shades his playfellow's reproachful face.
  Estranged through one transcendent deed
From common membership in mart,
In severance he is like a head
Pale after battle trunkless found apart.

VII.

But flood-tide comes though long the ebb,
Nor patience bides with passion long;
Like sightless orbs his thoughts are rolled
Arraigning heaven as compromised in wrong:
  To second causes why appeal?
Vain parleying here with fellow clods.
To you, Arch Principals, I rear

My quarrel, for this quarrel is with gods.
  Shall just men long to quit your world?
It is aspersion of your reign;
Your marbles in the temple stand—
Yourselves as stony and invoked in vain?
  Ah, bear with one quite overborne,
Olympians, if he chide ye now;
Magnanimous be even though he rail
And hard against ye set the bleaching brow.
  If conscience doubt, she'll next recant.
What basis then? O, tell at last,
Are earnest natures staggering here
But fatherless shadows from no substance cast?
  Yea, *are* ye, gods? Then ye, 'tis ye
Should show what touch of tie ye may,
Since ye, too, if not wrung are wronged
By grievous misconceptions of your sway.
  But deign, some little sign be given—
Low thunder in your tranquil skies;
Me reassure, nor let me be
Like a lone dog that for a master cries.

VIII.

  Men's moods, as frames, must yield to years,
And turns the world in fickle ways;

Corinth recalls Timoleon—ay,
And plumes him forth, but yet with schooling
    phrase.
  On Sicily's fields, through arduous wars,
A peace he won whose rainbow spanned
The isle redeemed; and he was hailed
Deliverer of that fair colonial land.
  And Corinth clapt: Absolved, and more!
Justice in long arrears is thine:
Not slayer of thy brother, no,
But savior of the state, Jove's soldier, man
    divine.
  Eager for thee thy City waits:
Return! with bays we dress your door.
But he, the Isle's loved guest, reposed,
And never for Corinth left the adopted shore.

AFTER THE PLEASURE PARTY.

LINES TRACED

UNDER AN IMAGE OF

AMOR THREATENING.

Fear me, virgin whosoever
Taking pride from love exempt,
Fear me, slighted. Never, never
Brave me, nor my fury tempt:
Downy wings, but wroth they beat
Tempest even in reason's seat.

BEHIND the house the upland falls
 With many an odorous tree—
White marbles gleaming through green halls,
Terrace by terrace, down and down,
And meets the starlit Mediterranean Sea.

'Tis Paradise. In such an hour
Some pangs that rend might take release.
Nor less perturbed who keeps this bower
Of balm, nor finds balsamic peace?
From whom the passionate words in vent
After long revery's discontent?

Tired of the homeless deep,
Look how their flight yon hurrying billows urge,
Hitherward but to reap
Passive repulse from the iron-bound verge!
Insensate, can they never know
'Tis mad to wreck the impulsion so?

An art of memory is, they tell:
But to forget! forget the glade
Wherein Fate sprung Love's ambuscade,

To flout pale years of cloistral life
And flush me in this sensuous strife.
'Tis Vesta struck with Sappho's smart.
No fable her delirious leap:
With more of cause in desperate heart,
Myself could take it—but to sleep!·

Now first I feel, what all may ween,
That soon or late, if faded e'en,
One's sex asserts itself. Desire,
The dear desire through love to sway,
Is like the Geysers that aspire—
Through cold obstruction win their fervid way.
But baffled here—to take disdain,
To feel rule's instinct, yet not reign;
To dote, to come to this drear shame—
Hence the winged blaze that sweeps my soul
Like prairie fires that spurn control,
Where withering weeds incense the flame.

And kept I long heaven's watch for this,
Contemning love, for this, even this?
O terrace chill in Northern air,
O reaching ranging tube I placed
Against yon skies, and fable chased
Till, fool, I hailed for sister there

Starred Cassiopea in Golden Chair.
In dream I throned me, nor I saw
In cell the idiot crowned with straw.

And yet, ah yet scarce ill I reigned,
Through self-illusion self-sustained,
When now—enlightened, undeceived—
What gain I barrenly bereaved!
Than this can be yet lower decline—
Envy and spleen, can these be mine?

The peasant girl demure that trod
Beside our wheels that climbed the way,
And bore along a blossoming rod
That looked the sceptre of May-Day—
On her—to fire this petty hell,
His softened glance how moistly fell!
The cheat! on briars her buds were strung;
And wiles peeped forth from mien how meek.
The innocent bare-foot! young, so young!
To girls, strong man's a novice weak.
To tell such beads! And more remain,
Sad rosary of belittling pain.

When after lunch and sallies gay
Like the Decameron folk we lay

In sylvan groups ; and I——let be !
O, dreams he, can he dream that one
Because not roseate feels no sun ?
The plain lone bramble thrills with Spring
As much as vines that grapes shall bring.

Me now fair studies charm no more.
Shall great thoughts writ, or high themes sung
Damask wan cheeks—unlock his arm
About some radiant ninny flung ?
How glad with all my starry lore,
I'd buy the veriest wanton's rose
Would but my bee therein repose.

Could I remake me ! or set free
This sexless bound in sex, then plunge
Deeper than Sappho, in a lunge
Piercing Pan's paramount mystery !
For, Nature, in no shallow surge
Against thee either sex may urge,
Why hast thou made us but in halves—
Co-relatives ? This makes us slaves.
If these co-relatives never meet
Self-hood itself seems incomplete.
And such the dicing of blind fate

Few matching halves here meet and mate.
What Cosmic jest or Anarch blunder
The human integral clove asunder
And shied the fractions through life's gate?

Ye stars that long your votary knew
Rapt in her vigil, see me here!
Whither is gone the spell ye threw
When rose before me Cassiopea?
Usurped on by love's stronger reign—
But lo, your very selves do wane:
Light breaks—truth breaks! Silvered no more,
But chilled by dawn that brings the gale
Shivers yon bramble above the vale,
And disillusion opens all the shore.

One knows not if Urania yet
The pleasure-party may forget;
Or whether she lived down the strain
Of turbulent heart and rebel brain;
For Amor so resents a slight,
And her's had been such haught disdain,
He long may wreak his boyish spite,
And boy-like, little reck the pain.

One knows not, no.   But late in Rome
(For queens discrowned a congruous home)
Entering Albani's porch she stood
Fixed by an antique pagan stone
Colossal carved.   No anchorite seer,
Not Thomas a Kempis, monk austere,
Religious more are in their tone;
Yet far, how far from Christian heart
That form august of heathen Art.
Swayed by its influence, long she stood,
Till surged emotion seething down,
She rallied and this mood she won:

Languid in frame for me,
To-day by Mary's convent shrine,
Touched by her picture's moving plea
In that poor nerveless hour of mine,
I mused—A wanderer still must grieve.
Half I resolved to kneel and believe,
Believe and submit, the veil take on.
But thee, armed Virgin! less benign,
Thee now I invoke, thou mightier one.
Helmeted woman—if such term
Befit thee, far from strife
Of that which makes the sexual feud
And clogs the aspirant life—

O self-reliant, strong and free,
Thou in whom power and peace unite,
Transcender! raise me up to thee,
Raise me and arm me!

                              Fond appeal.
For never passion peace shall bring,
Nor Art inanimate for long
Inspire. Nothing may help or heal
While Amor incensed remembers wrong.
Vindictive, not himself he'll spare;
For scope to give his vengeance play
Himself he'll blaspheme and betray.

Then for Urania, virgins everywhere,
O pray! Example take too, and have care.

THE NIGHT-MARCH.

WITH banners furled, and clarions mute,
    An army passes in the night;
And beaming spears and helms salute
    The dark with bright.

In silence deep the legions stream,
    With open ranks, in order true;
Over boundless plains they stream and gleam—
    No chief in view!

Afar, in twinkling distance lost,
    (So legends tell) he lonely wends
And back through all that shining host
    His mandate sends.

THE RAVAGED VILLA.

IN shards the sylvan vases lie,
    Their links of dance undone,
And brambles wither by thy brim,
    Choked fountain of the sun!
The spider in the laurel spins,
    The weed exiles the flower:
And, flung to kiln, Apollo's bust
    Makes lime for Mammon's tower.

THE MARGRAVE'S BIRTHNIGHT.

UP from many a sheeted valley,
　　From white woods as well,
Down too from each fleecy upland
Jingles many a bell

Jovial on the work-sad horses
Hitched to runners old
Of the toil-worn peasants sledging
Under sheepskins in the cold;

Till from every quarter gathered
Meet they on one ledge,
There from hoods they brush the snow off
Lighting from each sledge

Full before the Margrave's castle,
Summoned there to cheer
On his birth-night, in mid-winter,
Kept year after year.

O the hall, and O the holly !
Tables line each wall ;
Guests as holly-berries plenty,
But—no host withal !

May his people feast contented
While at head of board
Empty throne and vacant cover
Speak the absent lord ?

Minstrels enter. And the stewards
Serve the guests ; and when,
Passing there the vacant cover,
Functiorally then

Old observance grave they offer ;
But no Margrave fair,
In his living aspect gracious,
Sits responsive there ;

No, and never guest once marvels,
None the good lord name,
Scarce they mark void throne and cover—
Dust upon the same.

Mindless as to what importeth
Absence such in hall ;

Tacit as the plough-horse feeding
In the palfrey's stall.

Ah, enough for toil and travail,
If but for a night
Into wine is turned the water,
Black bread into white.

MAGIAN WINE.

A MULETS gemmed, to Miriam dear,
    Adown in liquid mirage gleam;
Solomon's Syrian charms appear,
    Opal and ring supreme.
The rays that light this Magian Wine
Thrill up from semblances divine.

And, seething through the rapturous wave,
What low Elysian anthems rise:
Sibylline inklings blending rave,
    Then lap the verge with sighs.
Delirious here the oracles swim
Ambiguous in the beading hymn.

THE
GARDEN OF METRODORUS.

THE Athenians mark the moss-grown gate
    And hedge untrimmed that hides the
    haven green :
  And who keeps here his quiet state?
  And shares he sad or happy fate
Where never foot-path to the gate is seen?

Here none come forth, here none go in,
Here silence strange, and dumb seclusion dwell :
  Content from loneness who may win?
  And is this stillness peace or sin
Which noteless thus apart can keep its dell?

THE NEW ZEALOT TO THE SUN.

PERSIAN, you rise
    Aflame from climes of sacrifice
  Where adulators sue,
And prostrate man, with brow abased,
Adheres to rites whose tenor traced
  All worship hitherto.

Arch type of sway,
Meetly your over-ruling ray
  You fling from Asia's plain,
Whence flashed the javelins abroad
Of many a wild incursive horde
  Led by some shepherd Cain.

Mid terrors dinned
Gods too came conquerors from your Ind,
  The brood of Bramha throve;
They came like to the scythed car,
Westward they rolled their empire far,
  Of night their purple wove.

Chemist, you breed
In orient climes each sorcerous weed
  That energizes dream—
Transmitted, spread in myths and creeds,
Houris and hells, delirious screeds
  And Calvin's last extreme.

What though your light
In time's first dawn compelled the flight
  Of Chaos' startled clan,
Shall never all your darted spears
Disperse worse Anarchs, frauds and fears,
  Sprung from these weeds to man?

But Science yet
An effluence ampler shall beget,
    And power beyond your play—
Shall quell the shades you fail to rout,
Yea, searching every secret out
    Elucidate your ray.

THE WEAVER.

FOR years within a mud-built room
    For Arva's shrine he weaves the shawl,
Lone wight, and at a lonely loom,
His busy shadow on the wall.

The face is pinched, the form is bent,
No pastime knows he nor the wine,
Recluse he lives and abstinent
Who weaves for Arva's shrine.

LAMIA'S SONG.

DESCEND, descend !
 Pleasant the downward way—
From your lonely Alp
With the wintry scalp
To our myrtles in valleys of May.
 Wend then, wend :
Mountaineer, descend !
And more than a wreath shall repay.
 Come, ah come !
With the cataracts come,
That hymn as they roam
How pleasant the downward way !

IN A GARRET.

GEMS and jewels let them heap—
 Wax sumptuous as the Sophi :
For me, to grapple from Art's deep
 One dripping trophy !

MONODY.

TO have known him, to have loved him
    After loneness long;
And then to be estranged in life,
    And neither in the wrong;
And now for death to set his seal—
    Ease me, a little ease, my song!

By wintry hills his hermit-mound
    The sheeted snow-drifts drape,
And houseless there the snow-bird flits
    Beneath the fir-trees' crape:
Glazed now with ice the cloistral vine
    That hid the shyest grape.

LONE FOUNTS.

THOUGH fast youth's glorious fable flies,
    View not the world with worldling's eyes;
Nor turn with weather of the time.
Foreclose the coming of surprise:
Stand where Posterity shall stand;

Stand where the Ancients stood before,
And, dipping in lone founts thy hand,
Drink of the never-varying lore :
Wise once, and wise thence evermore.

THE BENCH OF BOORS.

IN bed I muse on Tenier's boors,
Embrowned and beery losels all :
  A wakeful brain
  Elaborates pain :
Within low doors the slugs of boors
Laze and yawn and doze again.

In dreams they doze, the drowsy boors,
Their hazy hovel warm and small :
  Thought's ampler bound
  But chill is found :
Within low doors the basking boors
Snugly hug the ember-mound.

Sleepless, I see the slumberous boors
Their blurred eyes blink, their eyelids fall :
  Thought's eager sight
  Aches—overbright !
Within low doors the boozy boors
Cat-naps take in pipe-bowl light.

THE ENTHUSIAST.

" Though He slay me
yet will I trust in Him."

SHALL hearts that beat no base retreat
　　In youth's magnanimous years—
Ignoble hold it, if discreet
　　When interest tames to fears;
Shall spirits that worship light
　　Perfidious deem its sacred glow,
　　Recant, and trudge where worldlings go,
Conform and own them right?

Shall Time with creeping influence cold
　　Unnerve and cow? the heart
Pine for the heartless ones enrolled
　　With palterers of the mart?
Shall faith abjure her skies,
　　Or pale probation blench her down
　　To shrink from Truth so still, so lone
Mid loud gregarious lies?

Each burning boat in Cæsar's rear,
　　Flames—No return through me!
So put the torch to ties though dear,
　　If ties but tempters be.

Nor cringe if come the night:
  Walk through the cloud to meet the pall,
  Though light forsake thee, never fall
From fealty to light.

ART.

IN placid hours well-pleased we dream
    Of many a brave unbodied scheme.
But form to lend, pulsed life create,
What unlike things must meet and mate:
A flame to melt—a wind to freeze;
Sad patience—joyous energies;
Humility—yet pride and scorn;
Instinct and study; love and hate;
Audacity—reverence. These must mate,
And fuse with Jacob's mystic heart,
To wrestle with the angel—Art.

BUDDHA.

" For what is your life? It is
even a vapor that appeareth for a
little time and then vanisheth away."

SWOONING swim to less and less
  Aspirant to nothingness!
Sobs of the worlds, and dole of kinds
  That dumb endurers be—
Nirvana! absorb us in your skies,
  Annul us into thee.

C＿＿＿＿＿'S LAMENT.

HOW lovely was the light of heaven,
  What angels leaned from out the sky
In years when youth was more than wine
And man and nature seemed divine
Ere yet I felt that youth must die.

  Ere yet I felt that youth must die
How insubstantial looked the earth,
Alladin-land! in each advance,
Or here or there, a new romance;
I never dreamed would come a dearth.

And nothing then but had its worth,
Even pain. Yes, pleasure still and pain
In quick reaction made of life
A lovers' quarrel, happy strife
In youth that never comes again.

But will youth never come again?
Even to his grave-bed has he gone,
And left me lone to wake by night
With heavy heart that erst was light?
O, lay it at his head—a stone!

SHELLEY'S VISION.

WANDERING late by morning seas
　　When my heart with pain was low—
Hate the censor pelted me—
Deject I saw my shadow go.

In elf-caprice of bitter tone
I too would pelt the pelted one :
At my shadow I cast a stone.

When lo, upon that sun-lit ground
I. saw the quivering phantom take
The likeness of St Stephen crowned :
Then did self-reverence awake.

FRAGMENTS OF A LOST

GNOSTIC POEM

OF THE 12TH CENTURY.

*   *   *   *

FOUND a family, build a state,
    The pledged event is still the same :
Matter in end will never abate
His ancient brutal claim.

*   *   *   *

Indolence is heaven's ally here,
And energy the child of hell :
The Good Man pouring from his pitcher clear,
But brims the poisoned well.

THE MARCHIONESS OF BRIN-VILLIERS.

HE toned the sprightly beam of morning
   With twilight meek of tender eve,
Brightness interfused with softness,
   Light and shade did weave:
And gave to candor equal place
With mystery starred in open skies;
And, floating all in sweetness, made
   Her fathomless mild eyes.

THE AGE OF THE ANTONINES.

WHILE faith forecasts millenial years
   Spite Europe's embattled lines,
Back to the Past one glance be cast—
   The Age of the Antonines!
O summit of fate, O zenith of time
When a pagan gentleman reigned,
And the olive was nailed to the inn of the
      world
Nor the peace of the just was feigned.
   A halcyon Age, afar it shines,
Solstice of Man and the Antonines.

Hymns to the nations' friendly gods
Went up from the fellowly shrines,
No demagogue beat the pulpit-drum
   In the Age of the Antonines!
The sting was not dreamed to be taken from
    death,
No Paradise pledged or sought,
But they reasoned of fate at the flowing feast,
Nor stifled the fluent thought.
   We sham, we shuffle while faith declines—
They were frank in the Age of the Antonines.

Orders and ranks they kept degree,
Few felt how the parvenu pines,
No law-maker took the lawless one's fee
   In the Age of the Antonines!
Under law made will the world reposed
And the ruler's right confessed,
For the heavens elected the Emperor then,
The foremost of men the best.
   Ah, might we read in America's signs
The Age restored of the Antonines.

HERBA SANTA.

I.

AFTER long wars when comes release
      Not olive wands proclaiming peace
An import dearer share
Than stems of Herba Santa hazed
      In autumn's Indian air.
Of moods they breathe that care disarm,
They pledge us lenitive and calm.

II.

Shall code or creed a lure afford
To win all selves to Love's accord?
When Love ordained a supper divine
      For the wide world of man,
What bickerings o'er his gracious wine!
      Then strange new feuds began.

Effectual more in lowlier way,
      Pacific Herb, thy sensuous plea
The bristling clans of Adam sway
      At least to fellowship in thee!

Before thine altar tribal flags are furled,
Fain woulds't thou make one hearthstone of
   the world.

III.

To scythe, to sceptre, pen and hod—
   Yea, sodden laborers dumb;
To brains overplied, to feet that plod,
In solace of the *Truce of God*
   The Calumet has come!

IV.

Ah for the world ere Raleigh's find
   Never that knew this suasive balm
That helps when Gilead's fails to heal,
   Helps by an interserted charm.

Insinuous thou that through the nerve
   Windest the soul, and so canst win
   Some from repinings, some from sin,
The Church's aim thou dost subserve.

The ruffled fag fordone with care
   And brooding, Gold would ease this pain:
Him soothest thou and smoothest down
   Till some content return again.

Even ruffians feel thy influence breed
  Saint Martin's summer in the mind,
They feel this last evangel plead,
As did the first, apart from creed,
  Be peaceful, man—be kind!

V.

Rejected once on higher plain,
O Love supreme, to come again
  Can this be thine?
Again to come, and win us too
  In likeness of a weed
That as a god didst vainly woo,
  As man more vainly bleed?

VI.

Forbear, my soul! and in thine Eastern
  chamber
  Rehearse the dream that brings the long
    release:
Through jasmine sweet and talismanic amber
  Inhaling Herba Santa in the passive Pipe of
    Peace.

FRUIT OF TRAVEL LONG AGO.

VENICE.

WITH Pantheist energy of will
    The little craftsman of the Coral Sea.
Strenuous in the blue abyss,
Up-builds his marvelous gallery
    And long arcade,
Erections freaked with many a fringe
    Of marble garlandry,
Evincing what a worm can do.

Laborious in a shallower wave,
    Advanced in kindred art,
A prouder agent proved Pan's might
When Venice rose in reefs of palaces.

IN A BYE-CANAL.

A SWOON of noon, a trance of tide
    The hushed siesta brooding wide
Like calms far off Peru;
No floating wayfarer in sight,
Dumb noon, and haunted like the night
    When Jael the wiled one slew.

A languid impulse from the oar
Plied by my indolent gondolier
Tinkles against a palace hoar,
   And, hark, response I hear !
A lattice clicks ; and lo, I see
Between the slats, mute summoning me,
What loveliest eyes of scintillation,
What basilisk glance of conjuration !

   Fronted I have, part taken the span
Of portents in nature and peril in man.
I have swum—I have been
Twixt the whale's black flukes and the white
     shark's fin ;
The enemy's desert have wandered in,
And there have turned, have turned and scanned,
Following me how noiselessly,
Envy and Slander, lepers hand in hand.
All this. But at the latticed eye—
" Hey ! Gondolier, you sleep, my man ;
Wake up !" And, shooting by, we ran ;
The while I mused, This, surely now,
Confutes the Naturalists, allow !
Sirens, true sirens verily be,
Sirens, waylayers in the sea.

Well, wooed by these same deadly misses,
Is it shame to run?
No! flee them did divine Ulysses,
  Brave, wise, and Venus' son.

PISA'S LEANING TOWER.

THE Tower in tiers of architraves,
    Fair circle over cirque,
A trunk of rounded colonades,
The maker's master-work,
Impends with all its pillared tribes,
And, poising them, debates:
It thinks to plunge—but hesitates;
Shrinks back—yet fain would slide;
Witholds itself—itself would urge;
Hovering, shivering on the verge,
  A would-be suicide!

IN A CHURCH OF PADUA.

IN vaulted place where shadows flit,
    An upright sombre box you see:
A door, but fast, and lattice none,
But punctured holes minutely small
In lateral silver panel square
Above a kneeling-board without,
Suggest an aim if not declare.

Who bendeth here the tremulous knee
No glimpse may get of him within,
And he immured may hardly see
The soul confessing there the sin;
Nor yields the low-sieved voice a tone
Whereby the murmurer may be known.

Dread diving-bell! In thee inurned
What hollows the priest must sound,
Descending into consciences
    Where more is hid than found.

MILAN CATHEDRAL.

THROUGH light green haze, a rolling sea
    Over gardens where redundance flows,
The fat old plain of Lombardy,
The White Cathedral shows.

Of Art the miracles
Its tribes of pinnacles
Gleam like to ice-peaks snowed; and higher,
Erect upon each airy spire
In concourse without end,
Statues of saints over saints ascend
Like multitudinous forks of fire.

What motive was the master-builder's here?
Why these synodic hierarchies given,
Sublimely ranked in marble sessions clear,
Except to signify the host of heaven.

PAUSILIPPO.

(*In the time of Bomba.*)

A HILL there is that laves its feet
        In Naples' bay and lifts its head
In jovial season, curled with vines.
Its name, in pristine years conferred
By settling Greeks, imports that none
Who take the prospect thence can pine,
For such the charm of beauty shown
Even sorrow's self they cheerful weened
Surcease might find and thank good Pan.

Toward that hill my landeau drew;
And there, hard by the verge, was seen
Two faces with such meaning fraught
One scarce could mark and straight pass on.

A man it was less hoar with time
Than bleached through strange immurement long,
Retaining still, by doom depressed,
Dim trace of some aspiring prime.

Seated he tuned a homely harp
Watched by a girl, whose filial mien
Toward one almost a child again,
Took on a staid maternal tone.
Nor might one question that the locks
Which in smoothed natural silvery curls
Fell on the bowed one's thread-bare coat
Betrayed her ministering hand.

Anon, among some ramblers drawn
A murmur rose "Tis Silvio, Silvio!"
With inklings more in tone suppressed
Touching his story, part recalled:
Clandestine arrest abrupt by night;
The sole conjecturable cause
The yearning in a patriot ode
Construed as treason; trial none;
Prolonged captivity profound;
Vain liberation late. All this,
With pity for impoverishment
And blight forestalling age's wane.

Hillward the quelled enthusiast turned,
Unmanned, made meek through strenuous wrong,
Preluding, faltering; then began,

But only thrilled the wire—no more,
The constant maid supplying voice,
Hinting by no ineloquent sign
That she was but his mouth-piece mere,
Himself too spiritless and spent.

Pausilippo, Pausilippo,
Pledging easement unto pain,
  Shall your beauty even solace
If one's sense of beauty wane?

Could light airs that round ye play
Waft heart-heaviness away
Or memory lull to sleep,
  Then, then indeed your balm
  Might Silvio becharm,
And life in fount would leap,
  Pausilippo!

Did not your spell invite,
  In moods that slip between,
  A dream of years serene,
And wake, to dash, delight—

Evoking here in vision
Fulfilment and fruition—
Nor mine, nor meant for man!
 Did hope not frequent share
 The mirage when despair
Overtakes the caravan,
  Me then your scene might move
  To break from sorrow's snare,
  And apt your name would prove,
   Pausilippo!

But I've looked upon your revel—
 It unravels not the pain:
Pausilippo, Pausilippo,
 Named benignly if in vain!

  It ceased. In low and languid tone
The tideless ripple lapped the passive shore;
As listlessly the bland untroubled heaven
Looked down as silver doled was silent given
In pity—futile as the ore!

THE ATTIC LANDSCAPE.

TOURIST, spare the avid glance
   That greedy roves the sight to see:
Little here of " Old Romance,"
   Or Picturesque of Tivoli.

No flushful tint the sense to warm—
Pure outline pale, a linear charm.
The clear-cut hills carved temples face,
Respond, and share their sculptural grace.

'Tis Art and Nature lodged together,
   Sister by sister, cheek to cheek ;
Such Art, such Nature, and such weather
   The All-in-All seems here a Greek.

THE SAME.

A CIRCUMAMBIENT spell it is,
   Pellucid on these scenes that waits,
Repose that does of Plato tell—
   Charm that his style authenticates.

THE PARTHENON.

I.

Seen aloft from afar.

ESTRANGED in site,
   Aerial gleaming, warmly white,
You look a suncloud motionless
In noon of day divine;
Your beauty charmed enhancement takes
In Art's long after-shine.

II.

Nearer viewed.

Like Lais, fairest of her kind,
In subtlety your form's defined—
The cornice curved, each shaft inclined,
While yet, to eyes that do but revel
   And take the sweeping view,
Erect this seems, and that a level,
   To line and plummet true.

Spinoza gazes; and in mind
Dreams that one architect designed
   Lais—and you!

III.

The Frieze.

What happy musings genial went
With airiest touch the chisel lent
　　To frisk and curvet light
Of horses gay—their riders grave—
Contrasting so in action brave
　　With virgins meekly bright,
Clear filing on in even tone
With pitcher each, one after one
　　Like water-fowl in flight.

IV.

The last Tile.

When the last marble tile was laid
The winds died down on all the seas ;
　　Hushed were the birds, and swooned the glade ;
　　Ictinus sat ; Aspasia said
" Hist !—Art's meridian, Pericles ! "

GREEK MASONRY.

JOINTS were none that mortar sealed :
      Together, scarce with line revealed,
The blocks in symmetry congealed.

GREEK ARCHITECTURE.

NOT magnitude, not lavishness,
      But Form—the Site ;
Not innovating wilfulness,
But reverence for the Archetype.

OFF CAPE COLONNA.

ALOOF they crown the foreland lone,
      From aloft they loftier rise—
Fair columns, in the aureola rolled
      From sunned Greek seas and skies.
They wax, sublimed to fancy's view,
A god-like group against the blue.

Over much like gods ! •Serene they saw
      The wolf-waves board the deck,
And headlong hull of Falconer,
      And many a deadlier wreck.

THE ARCHIPELAGO.

SAIL before the morning breeze
   The Sporads through and Cyclades
They look like isles of absentees—
       Gone whither?

You bless Apollo's cheering ray,
But Delos, his own isle, today
Not e'en a Selkirk there to pray
       God friend me!

Scarce lone these groups, scarce lone and bare
When Theseus roved a Raleigh there,
Each isle a small Virginia fair—
       Unravished.

Nor less through havoc fell they rue,
They still retain in outline true
Their grace of form when earth was new
       And primal.

But beauty clear, the frame's as yet,
Never shall make one quite forget
Thy picture, Pan, therein once set—
        Life's revel!

'Tis Polynesia reft of palms,
Seaward no valley breathes her balms—
Not such as musk thy rings of calms,
        Marquesas!

SYRA.

(*A Transmitted Reminiscence.*)

FLEEING from Scio's smouldering vines
    (Where when the sword its work had
  done
The Turk applied the torch) the Greek
Came here, a fugitive stript of goods,
Here to an all but tenantless isle,
Nor here in footing gained at first,
Felt safe. Still from the turbaned foe
Dreading the doom of shipwrecked men
Whom feline seas permit to land

Then pounce upon and drag them back,
For height they made, and prudent won
A cone-shaped fastness on whose flanks
With pains they pitched their eyrie camp,
Stone huts, whereto they wary clung ;
But, reassured in end, come down—
Multiplied through compatriots now,
Refugees like themselves forlorn—
And building along the water's verge
Begin to thrive ; and thriving more
When Greece at last flung off the Turk,
Make of the haven mere a mart.

I saw it in its earlier day—
Primitive, such an isled resort
As heartless Homer might have known
Wandering about the Ægean here.
Sheds ribbed with wreck-stuff faced the sea
Where goods in transit shelter found ;
And here and there a shanty-shop
Where Fez-caps, swords, tobacco, shawls
Pistols, and orient finery, Eve's—
(The spangles dimmed by hands profane)
Like plunder on a pirate's deck
Lay orderless in such loose way
As to suggest things ravished or gone astray.

Above a tented inn with fluttering flag
A sunburnt board announced Greek wine
In self-same text Anacreon knew,
Dispensed by one named " Pericles."
Got up as for the opera's scene,
Armed strangers, various, lounged or lazed,
Lithe fellows tall, with gold-shot eyes,
Sunning themselves as leopards may.

Off-shore lay xebecs trim and light,
And some but dubious in repute.
But on the strand, for docks were none,
What busy bees! no testy fry;
Frolickers, picturesquely odd,
With bales and oil-jars lading boats,
Lighters that served an anchored craft,
Each in his tasseled Phrygian cap,
Blue Eastern drawers and braided vest;
And some with features cleanly cut
As Proserpine's upon the coin.
Such chatterers all! like children gay
Who make believe to work, but play.

I saw, and how help musing too.
Here traffic's immature as yet:
Forever this juvenile fun hold out

And these light hearts? Their garb, their glee,
Alike profuse in flowing measure,
Alike inapt for serious work,
Blab of grandfather Saturn's prime
When trade was not, nor toil, nor stress,
But life was leisure, merriment, peace,
And lucre none and love was righteousness.

DISINTERMENT OF THE HERMES.

WHAT forms divine in adamant fair—
    Carven demigod and god,
And hero-marbles rivalling these,
Bide under Latium's sod,
Or lost in sediment and drift
Alluvial which the Grecian rivers sift.

To dig for these, O better far
Than raking arid sands
For gold more barren meetly theirs
Sterile, with brimming hands.

THE APPARITION.

*(The Parthenon uplifted on
its rock first challenging the view
on the approach to Athens.)*

ABRUPT the supernatural Cross,
    Vivid in startled air,
Smote the Emperor Constantine
And turned his soul's allegiance there.

With other power appealing down,
    Trophy of Adam's best !
If cynic minds you scarce convert,
You try them, shake them, or molest.

Diogenes, that honest heart,
    Lived ere your date began ;
Thee had he seen, he might have swerved
In mood nor barked so much at Man.

IN THE DESERT.

NEVER Pharoah's Night,
    Whereof the Hebrew wizards croon,
Did so the Theban flamens try
As me this veritable Noon.

Like blank ocean in blue calm
Undulates the ethereal frame;
In one flowing oriflamme
God flings his fiery standard out.

Battling with the Emirs fierce
Napoleon a great victory won,
Through and through his sword did pierce;
But, bayonetted by this sun
His gunners drop beneath the gun.

Holy, holy, holy Light!
Immaterial incandescence,
Of God the effluence of the essence,
Shekinah intolerably bright!

THE GREAT PYRAMID.

Your masonry—and is it man's?
More like some Cosmic artisan's.
Your courses as in strata rise,
Beget you do a blind surmise
        Like Grampians.

Far slanting up your sweeping flank
Arabs with Alpine goats may rank,
And there they find a choice of passes
Even like to dwarfs that climb the masses
        Of glaciers blank.

Shall lichen in your crevice fit?
Nay, sterile all and granite-knit:
Weather nor weather-stain ye rue,
But aridly you cleave the blue
        As lording it.

Morn's vapor floats beneath your peak,
Kites skim your side with pinion weak;
To sand-storms battering, blow on blow,
Raging to work your overthrow,
        You—turn the cheek.

All elements unmoved you stem,
Foursquare you stand and suffer them :
Time's future infinite you dare,
While, for the past, 'tis you that wear
   Eld's diadem.

Slant from your inmost lead the caves
And labyrinths rumored. These who braves
And penetrates (old palmers said)
Comes out afar on deserts dead
   And, dying, raves.

Craftsmen, in dateless quarries dim,
Stones formless into form did trim,
Usurped on Nature's self with Art,
And bade this dumb I AM to start,
   Imposing him.

L' ENVOI.

THE RETURN

OF THE SIRE DE NESLE.

A. D. 16—

My towers at last! These rovings end,
Their thirst is slaked in larger dearth:
The yearning infinite recoils,
  For terrible is earth.

Kaf thrusts his snouted crags through fog:
Araxes swells beyond his span,
And knowledge poured by pilgrimage
  Overflows the banks of man.

But thou, my stay, thy lasting love
One lonely good, let this but be!
Weary to view the wide world's swarm,
  But blest to fold but thee.